To Katarina —
Kristin Korda
Saco, ME
Age 11
Grade 6

THE THREE WISHES

MARGOT ZEMACH

THE THREE WISHES

· AN OLD STORY ·

FARRAR, STRAUS & GIROUX

New York

Copyright © 1986 by Margot Zemach
All rights reserved
Library of Congress catalog card number: 86-80956
Published in Canada by HarperCollins*CanadaLtd*
Color separations by Offset Separations Corp.
Printed in the United States of America
by Horowitz/Rae Book Manufacturers
Designed by Atha Tehon
First edition, 1986
Second printing, 1993

For Cybele, Ariella & Talya

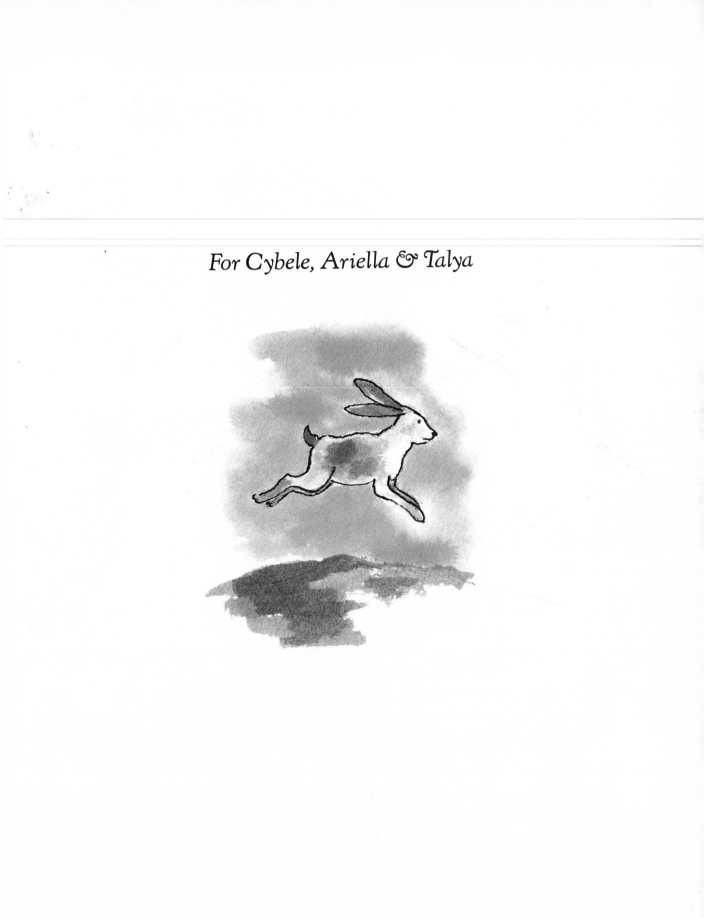

LONG AGO, a man and his wife lived peacefully at the edge of a great forest. All the year round, they worked together as woodcutters.

Every morning, at sunrise, they went into the forest, where they cut trees and branches into logs. At sunset, they carried them home. But no matter how hard or how long they worked, they often went hungry.

Early one morning, as they were working in the forest, they heard a faint voice calling: "Help, help, someone help me!" The voice seemed to be coming from an old tree that had fallen nearby.

The man and his wife ran to the tree. There on the ground lay a small imp kicking his legs. His tail was caught under the fallen tree! "Help, help," the imp cried weakly.

"We'll help you gladly," the man and his wife said together. And they pushed and pushed till the tree rolled off.

The imp sprang straight up into the air, joyfully twirling his tail. "A hundred thanks for your kindness," he said. "I have been lying here in misery ever since this tree fell. To thank you for saving me, I will give you three wishes. There are only three, so wish wisely, my friends—and goodbye!" Then he flew up among the branches and disappeared.

The man and his wife were delighted with their good luck. All that cold day, they were warmed by thoughts of the three wishes that would soon be theirs. "We might wish for fine clothes and silver," thought the wife, "or even for a grand house with flower gardens and fruit trees."

In the evening, as they trudged home, the man thought: "We might wish for a donkey to carry this wood, or even a horse and cart to ride in."

"That's so, that's so," he said to himself, and his bundle of wood seemed to grow lighter.

When they got home, the man and his wife settled down to
talk about their three wishes. "We might wish for fine clothes
and silver," said the wife, "or a grand house with beautiful flower
gardens and fruit trees."

"Or we might wish for a donkey to carry the wood, or even a
horse and cart to ride in ourselves," said the man.

"Or we might wish for a great chest of jewels," said the wife.

"Or even a mountain of gold coins!" said the man.

"We might wish never to go hungry again," said the wife.

"That's so, that's so," said the man. "But just now I wish we
had a pan of sausages for our dinner."

No sooner said than done. That very instant, a pan of sau-sages appeared, sizzling and smoking on the fire.

"Oh, you fool!" cried the wife. "Look what you've done! How I wish those sausages were hanging from your big nose!"

No sooner said than done. The sausages leaped from the pan and hung heavily from the man's nose.

"Oh, wife, see what you've done!" he cried. "Who's the fool now?"

The man and his wife tried every which way to get the sausages off. But, pull and tug as they might, all their efforts were useless. The sausages remained hanging from the poor man's nose.

Finally, too tired to move, the man and his wife slumped down before the fire.

They thought with longing of their one last wish. Should it be the donkey to carry the wood, the horse and cart to ride in together, the grand house, the fine clothes and jewels, or the mountain of gold coins? Any one of these wishes could still be theirs.

But what would be the good of it if the man must live his whole life with sausages hanging from his nose?

So they joined hands, and with their last wish they wished the sausages OFF.

No sooner said than done! The sausages were back in the pan, sizzling and smoking and smelling delicious.

So the man and his wife sat down cheerfully to a fine dinner.

"Well now, we've not done too badly," said the wife.

"That's so, that's so!" the man agreed.